DINNER FROM DIRT

TEN MEALS KIDS CAN GROW & COOK

Emily Scott and Catherine Duffy
Illustrations by Denise Kirby

Salt Lake City

First edition

02 01 00 99 98 5 4 3 2 1

This is a Gibbs Smith Junior book,
published by Gibbs Smith, Publisher
P.O. Box 667
Layton, Utah 84041

Book design by Denise Kirby

Printed in China

Note: Some of the activities suggested in this book require adult assistance and supervision, as noted throughout. The publisher and authors assume no responsibility for any damage or injuries incurred while performing any of the activities in this book nor for their results.

Library of Congress Cataloging-in-Publication Data

Scott, Emily, 1949-
Dinner from dirt: ten meals kids can grow and cook / by Emily Scott and Catherine Duffy: illustrated by Denise Kirby. —1st ed.
p. cm.
ISBN 0-87905-840-4
1. Cookery (Vegetables)—Juvenile literature. 2. Vegetable gardening—Juvenile literature.
I. Duffy, Catherine, 1964– . II. Denise Kirby, 1955– . III. Title.

TX801.S37 1998
781.62'13'0092—dc21 97–33283
CIP
AC

CONTENTS

THE "SCOOP" ON DIRT

Did you have cereal for breakfast? Maybe a sandwich for lunch? How about some rice or potatoes with dinner? Then you know what it's like to get your meals from dirt.

Okay, so you're not exactly plucking food from the mud you drag in on your shoes. But many of the food products we eat are grown in the earth—planted, watered, and tended in the same stuff stuck to the bottom of your shoes.

Have you ever wondered how the pizza you eat for lunch or the salad you have with dinner arrives at your table? You might buy the food from a store or restaurant, which may buy that food from a supplier, which may buy that food from a manufacturer, which may . . . well, you get the picture. But at the very beginning of that process—before all the buying and selling— there was dirt. Something had to be planted in that dirt to create the food.

Of course, some of the foods we eat are artificially made, and some come from animals. But you would probably be surprised at the variety and amount of food you can grow in dirt.

Think about your favorite foods. What if you could grow many of the ingredients to make them in your own backyard? With this book, the right soil, and the right care of your "crops," you can grow many plants in a small backyard plot, in a window box, in pots and buckets, or in any spare patch of earth.

Foods that you grow yourself and pick ripe from your garden are more flavorful and more healthful than what you can buy. You prepare the soil, so you know what gets put into it—and what doesn't. You won't have to guess what the ingredients are in the foods on your plate.

So grab your gardening gloves and your oven mitts—and get ready to dive into some dirt!

DECIDING WHAT TO PLANT

This is probably the toughest part of gardening. When you go to a nursery or garden store to buy plants for the garden, everything looks so good that it's not easy to take home just a few plants!

If you're a first-time gardener, we suggest that you buy plants for fruits and vegetables that you already like to eat. That way, you know you're going to like what grows in your garden.

Ten favorite meals are discussed in the pages that follow. For each one, we list the basic foods that you will need to make these foods from scratch. Each recipe will serve about four people—two adults and two kids—so you should add or subtract from the given amounts depending on how many people you will be serving. We'll show how you can arrange the plants in your garden plot and estimate the time it will take your "meal" to grow. (Too bad you can't plant it in the morning and eat it for supper that night, huh?) Then we'll give recipes and directions for turning your homegrown produce into the best meals you'll ever eat. And the biggest reward: you will have done it yourself!

PREPARING THE PLOT

The three things needed for growing garden goodies are:

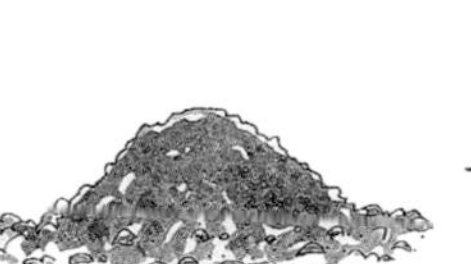
Dirt

Sunlight

Water

Almost any **dirt** will do, but it needs to be in good condition. The most important job before planting a garden is to *till* the soil. This means to "work" the dirt with a shovel or garden fork by digging it up and turning it over, time and time again. Do this until there are no sizable dirt clods. The soil should be loose to a depth of about eight to twelve inches.

Your gardening dirt can be either in the ground,or in pots or other containers.

If you have space in the ground, then you already have dirt. If you want to plant your garden in pots, you can either dig some dirt from your yard (but only from a spot approved by the owner of the yard—don't dig up Mom's petunias!) or you can buy potting soil from the store. If you use dirt from your yard, be sure to till the soil as described above before filling the pots. Adding peat moss (you can get this at a garden store or nursery), dead leaves, or grass clippings to garden soil for pots is a good idea. These "soil boosters" will help keep the dirt from packing in too tight.

If you're gardening in pots or containers, be sure to use large pots, not small ones. Try to imagine how big your plants will be when they are grown. The roots will be even bigger. So choose containers big enough to hold the roots. Give them plenty of room to grow. And make sure each container has a hole in the bottom for excess water to run out.

Garden plants need full **sunlight** for at least 8 hours of the day. If you choose a shady spot, you will be disappointed with the results.

Plants need **water**, but too much water can make the roots weak or lazy. To know when to water, dig about 3 to 4 inches down in the dirt with your finger. If it is dry, or mostly dry, give your plants some water. But if it is still wet, wait a day and check it again. Plant leaves sometimes wilt during the heat of the day, then revive at night, so it is best to check your plants for water in the morning.

HOW TO PLANT

If you're a first-time gardener, we suggest you choose a couple of your favorite foods from this book and follow the planting guide. For instance, if pizza is your favorite food, plant a Pizza Garden. See page 18 for which plants to buy and how to arrange them in a garden plot.

If you are an experienced gardener, you could probably manage a garden big enough to fix *all* ten meals in the book. You could plant a Pizza Garden right next to a Salad Garden and a Spud Garden. Keep adding space to your yard garden or add more containers to your patio garden.

SEEDS OR PLANTS? WHICH WAY IS BETTER?

The truth is that all vegetables can be grown from seed. But buying plants for some vegetables is a faster and surer means of getting a good start in the garden. Carrots, lettuce, and radishes will only be available as seeds. You can buy seed packets and plants from variety stores, grocery stores, or home and garden stores. Follow the planting directions on the seed packets.

However, other garden crops such as tomatoes and strawberries are much easier grown from plants that have been started in a nursery. Select the varieties recommended in our garden guides, or choose any variety you like. Take the plants home, prepare the soil, and transfer the plants from their starter pots to your bigger pots or ground plots.

To transfer a plant from a starter pot to its permanent home, first dig a hole in the ground for each plant or make holes in the dirt in your container garden. The holes should be as big around

as the starter pots. Pour about a cup of water into the hole and let it soak into the dirt. Then be sure the soil in the starter pot is wet. Tip the plant upside down in your hands like the picture shows, using one hand to hold the root ball and dirt together. Set aside the starter pot and work with both hands to place the plant in the hole.

A general rule for how deep to place the plants is this: Bury the root ball right up to where the first stem or leaves start. In fact, you can bury the first leaf. Push the dirt you dug from the hole loosely around the root ball. Then push the dirt firmly around the roots with both hands. This will squeeze any extra air from the hole.

(Roots exposed too long to air will die.) Give the plant a little more water. Keep the soil damp for the first week (or until the seeds sprout if you planted seeds). After that, water when the plants need it.

Now all you have to do is sit back, pull a few weeds now and then, water as needed, and watch your plants grow. If your plants are growing in too thick, "thin" them, or pull out one or two between the ones you leave. Be patient. In just 6 weeks, you'll start eating garden goodies that will explode with flavor when you bite into them.

TIMETABLE

In general, crops are planted in the spring, grown in the summer, and harvested in summer and fall. But you can make more than one planting of many crops and eat those vegetables all summer long and into the fall. Some expert gardeners measure the passing of the season by the rotating of crops.

Some plants will produce only for a week or two or the fruit will ripen all at once (marked SS). Other plants continue to produce for the rest of the growing season (marked LB). Some vegetables should be planted so they mature when the weather is cool in the early summer or fall (marked CW). Many vegetables can have multiple plantings a few weeks apart so you can eat them all season (marked MP).

Most garden plants should be put in the ground in between early April and late May, just after the last winter frost. (It's hard to tell which frost will be the last one of the year, so it pays to listen to the nightly weather reports for clues.) If you live in a warm state where there is never frost, March is still a good month for planting a summer garden. But you may be able to grow some things all year round.

The fastest meal to grow is salad (see page 14). You can begin eating salads from your garden (lettuce, spinach, radishes) about 45 days after planting. If you add second and third plantings of lettuce and other greens, your fresh salads will get even better as the summer goes on because you can add tomatoes, cucumbers, and carrots. Try starting a new planting of greens about one month after your first planting, but in a location that will receive a little bit of shade in early morning or evening. You can plant another row of spinach in late August for a fall crop. And new plantings of corn about three weeks apart will give

Here's the order in which a typical garden might bear fruit:

SS = short bearing season

LB = long bearing season

CW = cool weather

MP = can have multiple plantings

MAY

radishes (CW, SS)

JUNE

lettuce and other greens (MP)

spinach (CW, SS, MP)

JULY

herbs (LB)

beans (SS, MP)

sugar pod peas (SS)

cucumbers (LB)

zucchini (LB)

AUGUST

corn (SS, MP)

green onions (LB)

carrots (LB)

tomatoes (LB)

peppers (LB)

SEPTEMBER

onions (SS)

cabbage (LB, CW)

broccoli (CW)

potatoes (SS)

pumpkins (SS)

you corn on the cob over a couple of months instead of just a week or so.

Check with a nurseryman or expert gardener in your area to learn when the time is right for planting specific crops.

The food that will probably take the longest to grow is pumpkins—they won't be ready until late September. But serving your family or friends a sweet treat made from the pumpkin you grew will make you proud to be a gardener.

SAFETY TIPS

FOR THE GARDEN

Never use sharp garden tools without an adult present. Ask for instructions on how to use different tools before you begin. Demonstrate how responsible you are by working safely in the garden.

Don't use any chemical sprays or fertilizers without adult supervision.

Ask for help before placing any potted plants or window boxes on sills, ledges, porches, patios, etc. The containers should be on a level surface and heavy enough not to tip over easily.

Remember to use a hat and sunscreen if you're working outdoors.

Put away your tools (and your spilled dirt!) as soon as you're finished.

FOR THE KITCHEN

Never use sharp knives, the stove, or the oven without first asking permission from an adult and having supervision.

Be extra careful when chopping and slicing vegetables. Cut on a cutting board on a level surface, and hold steady the food you're cutting, with your fingertips in and away from the knife.

Be sure you use hot pads when moving hot pans. Keep the area around the stove and oven clear of towels and food wrappers, and roll up your shirtsleeves before you begin cooking.

Clean up spills when they happen, and clean up the kitchen when you're finished.

We'll put "safety first" signs like this throughout the book as reminders, but remember to use your noggin!

SANDWICH GARDEN

By the way, a sandwich is called a sandwich because of John Montagu, the fourth Earl of Sandwich. He was an Englishman who didn't like to stop playing cards in order to eat. So instead of eating from his plate, he put his meat inside his bread and held that with one hand and his cards in the other hand. You can be just as inventive with the meals you make!

Could the sandwich be the perfect meal? Consider this: there are millions of ways to make them, they're easy to transport, they're easy to clean up, and they have all the foods you need in one neat package. You can have simple peanut-butter-and-jelly sandwiches for picnics, foot-long submarine sandwiches for parties, elegant tomato-and-dill sandwiches with tea, and a stacked hero sandwich for a brown-bag lunch. The sandwich just might be the perfect idea for a meal!

Once you have that basic idea in your head (bread + filling), you can re-invent it in all sorts of ways. For example, tacos are basically sandwiches; you hold a corn tortilla shell filled with meat, cheese, lettuce, and tomatoes in your hand and eat it just like a sandwich. There are all kinds of outer shells you can choose for sandwiches: sliced bread, pita pockets, rolls, crepes, crackers, etc. And your garden will be a source for all sorts of fillings: lettuce, tomatoes, cucumbers, onions, peppers, green onions, and herbs.

THE SANDWICH GARDEN PLAN

THINGS TO GROW
Beefsteak tomatoes
Green peppers
Lettuce
Cucumbers
Red onions
Opal basil
Oregano

Part of the responsibility in having a garden is to use up all of the produce. This is something we owe to the land and to the Great Spirit of the Harvest. In times when goods and money have been in short supply, people have tried to follow the idea in this saying: Waste not, want not.

So, with that goal in mind, it's fun to keep an eye on the garden plants and pick each vegetable when it is at its peak of ripeness and flavor. Then, get creative and figure out how to use little bits of various vegetables.

Sandwiches are a good way to do this. If you have just one tomato that is ripe, you can slice it and use it on four or five sandwiches. You can do the same thing with other vegetables.

RECIPE
BLOOMING SANDWICHES

UTENSILS NEEDED

Cutting board
Paring knife
Table knife

THINGS TO BUY

Sandwich spreads
Bread
Meat
Cheese
Pickles

Everybody knows how to build a sandwich. The trick is thinking what to put on it. And the key to never getting bored with sandwiches is to find interesting breads and rolls. So, here are several combinations of possible ingredients. Take it from there!

PIZZAWICH

Stack the ingredients, then melt in the microwave for a minute.

English muffin half
Tomato slices
Mozzarella cheese
Pepperoni
Red peppers
Mushrooms
Oregano
Basil

BLT

Favorite bread, toasted
Bacon strips, cooked
Tomatoes, sliced
Lettuce
Mayonnaise

GARDENER'S DELIGHT

Favorite bread, sliced
Tomatoes, thick-sliced
Salad dressing
Salt and pepper to taste

ITALIAN COMBO

Submarine sandwich roll
Tomato slices
Salami
Provolone cheese
Green pepper rings
Red onion rings
Opal basil leaves
Italian salad dressing
Mayonnaise

SALSAWICH

Crusty white bread
Tomato, diced
Onion, diced
Cucumber, diced
Avocado, sliced
Cilantro leaves
Sprinkle of vinegar
Dash of oil

LUNCH POCKET

Pita bread, halved
Lettuce, slivered
Tomatoes, diced
Red onion, chopped
Cheese, grated
Avocado, diced
Ham or turkey, diced
Thousand Island dressing

SALAD GARDEN

Salads can be meals on their own or part of another meal, with as many different ingredients as you can imagine. And because you can grow so many salad ingredients yourself (almost all the good ones come from dirt), you never have to be bored eating the same kind of salad day after day! You can start with some basics: lettuce with some tomatoes and cucumbers on top, maybe. Then you can get inventive—how about a salad with no lettuce, and perhaps peppers and corn as the main ingredients? Or add chicken, tuna, bacon, nuts, or grains to spinach leaves for a chewy meal full of texture. How about arranging as many greens and vegetables as you can think of buffet-style, along with different kinds of dressings, and letting your guests serve themselves at your own salad bar?

Even better news: having fun mixing different colors (like the stoplight colors of peppers) and textures (like smooth cucumbers and rough carrots) means you're getting a good variety of vitamins and minerals, too.

Lettuce is an unhappy grower when the weather turns very hot. So plan on lettuce early in the summer. Then, rather than leaving that dirt empty after you have pulled all the lettuce, you can plant *second crops* such as potatoes, beans, onions, more corn, or carrots. And after the hottest days of summer, you can plant second or third crops of greens again—spinach, lettuce, and chard for autumn dishes. That way you'll get the most use—and most dinners—out of your dirt!

THE SALAD GARDEN PLAN

THINGS TO GROW
Lettuce
Spinach
Radishes
Cucumbers
Carrots
Peas
Green onions
Tomatoes
Cabbage (red or green)
Peppers (red, green, or yellow)

A wide variety of green leafy vegetables can be grown in the garden and are delicious in salads. Spinach is the green that can be planted earliest. It likes to grow in cool weather, so planting seeds in April (or right after the last frost) will give you fresh salad greens within 45 days. Leaf lettuce matures fast and can also be planted early in the growing season. Bibb lettuce makes a small, loose head of leaves. Check the seed packets in your area to see what other greens are available. Have you ever heard of dandelion leaves for salad? When they are young (before the flowers grow), dandelion leaves make a nice addition to other salad greens. But be sure not to pick them from a lawn that has been sprayed with chemicals!

RECIPE

SPRINKLER-FED SALAD WITH DRESSING

UTENSILS NEEDED:

- Jar for mixing the dressing
- Measuring cups & spoons

There are no rules here! Put on your creative chef's hat and make a mouth-watering salad for one or for ten. Pick any garden greens you want. Wash the leaves individually in cold water to remove dirt and bugs (yuk!). Then dry the leaves carefully between absorbent towels, or give them a little whirl in a salad spinner if you have one. Tear the leaves into bite-sized pieces and put into a serving bowl. If you plan to serve from the bowl, go ahead and add any other salad toppers you want (of course, washed and sliced into quarter-sized pieces).

Or, switch your chef's hat for an artist's chapeau and create individual salad plates, artfully arranged with colorful toppers on beds of greens. Arrange each plate a little differently to match the personality and tastes of the diner.

OTHER SALAD TASTIES FROM THE STORE

- Black olives
- Alfalfa sprouts
- Croutons
- Cheese
- Nuts or seeds
- Beets
- Fruit—oranges, pears, berries, apples
- Prepared dressing of your choice

POPPY SEED DRESSING

Delicious with a salad of leaf lettuce, fresh fruit, and thin-sliced rings of red onion. Remember to ask for help when using a blender or other electric appliance.

1/4 cup wine vinegar or fruit vinegar

1/2 cup honey

1 teaspoon dry mustard powder

1 tablespoon dehydrated onion flakes

1 tablespoon poppy seeds

1/3 cup vegetable oil

Place all ingredients except the oil into a blender. Put on the lid and blend for 5 to 10 seconds. Then, through the opening in the lid and while the blender is running, add the oil a little at a time. The dressing will thicken as the oil is added. Voilá! It's done.

NOTE: If your dressing tastes too sour, add another tablespoon of honey or sugar.

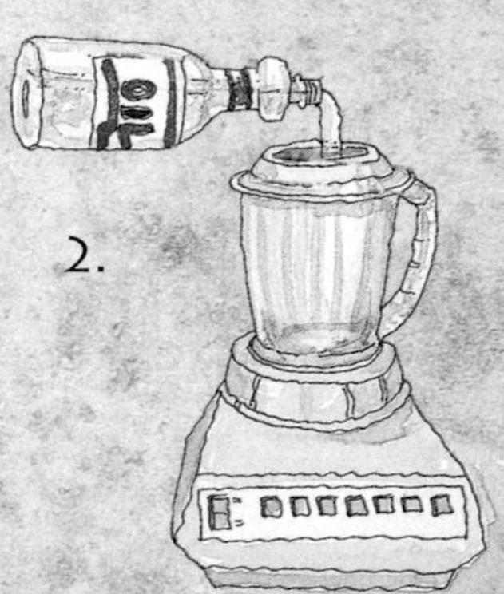

VINEGAR-AND-OIL DRESSING

For a light dressing that won't overpower the fresh garden greens, try this.

1/4 cup vinegar, any variety (balsamic vinegar makes a slightly sweet dressing)

1 teaspoon dry mustard powder

1/2 cup canola oil

Pour ingredients into a bottle, twist on the lid, and shake well just before pouring.

PIZZA GARDEN

THINGS TO GROW
Roma tomatoes
Green peppers
Sweet red peppers
Basil
Oregano

These garden toppings are also tasty on pizza:
Eggplant
Onion
Spinach

Peasant women in Italy used to break off pieces of bread while it was baking, flatten the dough, and then top it with whatever seasonings were on hand. (Nobody can resist testing the food while it's being prepared!) Tomatoes, once thought to be poisonous, weren't even added to those first circles of dough. And cheese wasn't added until 1889. That was when an Italian baker, making pizza for a queen, added mozzarella to a tomato-and-basil pizza to salute the colors of the Italian flag.

You already know that pizza is one of the easiest meals to eat (well, usually—unless it's overstuffed with cheese and toppings!). But it's also one of the easiest meals to cook. It's fast, you don't have to use a lot of pots and pans, and you can use almost any combination of ingredients you like.

Your pizza garden will take about three months to grow. The tomatoes will take the longest. So while you wait for your garden to grow, you can practice making pizza with store-bought ingredients. That way, by the time your tomatoes are ready for picking, you'll be an expert pizzamaker. (But you should still probably check with Mom before you start tossing the dough in the air.)

THE PIZZA GARDEN PLAN

Roma tomatoes are best for pizza because they are meatier (have more flesh, fewer seeds, and less juice) than other varieties. But any variety of tomato will work for pizza. If the kind you select seems too juicy for pizza, just slice off one end of the tomato, remove some seeds, and let some juice run out before you finish slicing the tomato for your pizza.

RECIPE

PLANTED PIZZA

UTENSILS NEEDED:

Medium bowl

Baking sheet of any shape

Fork

Sharp knife

Cutting board

NO-WAIT, NO-RISE PIZZA DOUGH

(Enough dough for two large, rectangular baking sheets)

2 cups lukewarm water

4 tablespoons sugar

1 tablespoon active dry yeast

4 tablespoons vegetable oil

5 cups flour

2 teaspoons salt

Yellow cornmeal

Put water, sugar, and yeast in a medium mixing bowl. Stir together, then let sit five minutes while the yeast "proofs" (begins to grow). Add oil, flour, and salt. Mix with a fork or spoon until all the flour is blended in.

Do not knead. Do not let rise.

Lightly oil baking pans of your choice. You can sprinkle yellow cornmeal over the oiled surface to help keep the pizza crust from sticking.

Divide dough into workable-sized pieces (about the size of a baseball for a small pizza; large grapefruit size for a large pizza with thin crust). Pat each piece into desired pizza shapes right on the pan. Work from the center out to the edges to get the crust's thickness as even as possible.

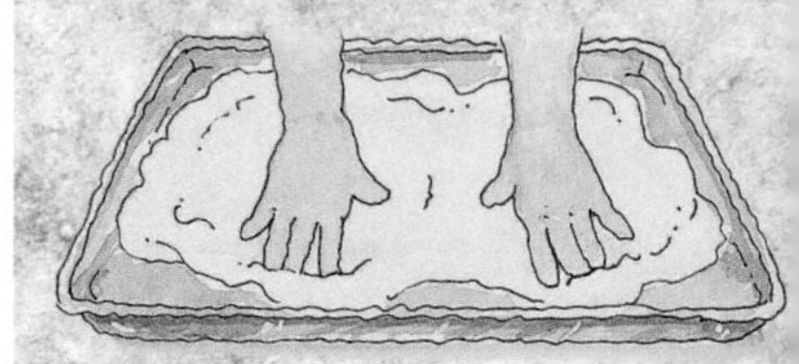

Remember, the dough will rise when you bake it.

When the crust is the size and shape you

want it, roll or pinch the edges up to make a lip so the tomato sauce won't run off.

TOPPING THE PIZZA

Mix the oregano into tomato sauce, then spread the sauce onto prepared crust with the back of a spoon. Sprinkle generous amounts of cheese over the sauce. Add all other toppings. Finish with a sprinkle of cheese.

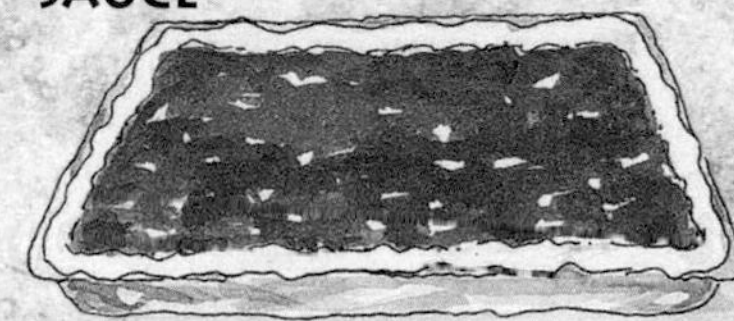

CHEESE

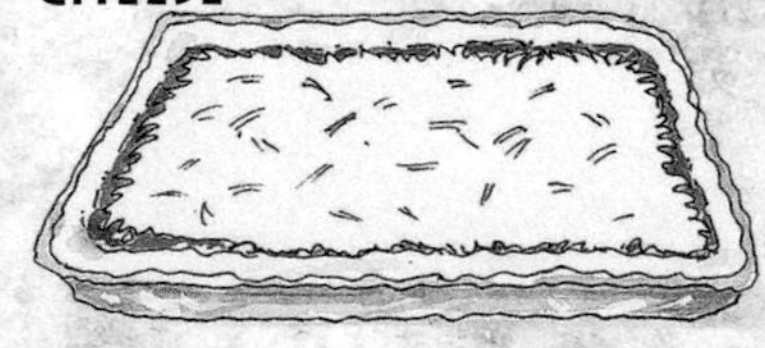

TOPPINGS

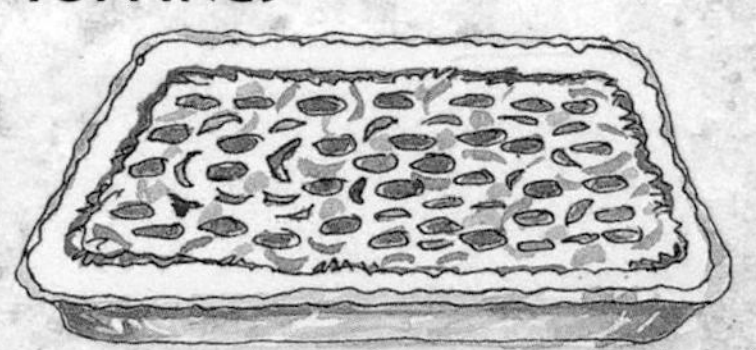

However, if you have a thick crust, hold off on the toppings. Bake it 20 to 25 minutes at 350 to 400 degrees, just until the crust begins to brown. Then remove from oven, let cool just a little, and add your favorite toppings. Return to oven until cheese bubbles and starts to turn brown.

If you have a thin crust, add toppings before baking. Bake 25 minutes or so at 375 to 400 degrees, until cheese bubbles and starts to turn brown.

When the baking is done, slice pizza into wedges or rectangles and serve—maybe with a **Garden Salad**! (See Salad Garden, page 14.)

TOPPINGS

Tomato sauce

Oregano (fresh leaves or dried)

Basil (fresh leaves or dried)

Cheese, grated (any variety: mozzarella, Swiss, cheddar/jack blend, feta)

Tomatoes (fresh), sliced

Green and red peppers, cut into strips

Any other items of your choice

OPTIONAL TOPPINGS

Olives

Pineapple

Mushrooms (fresh or canned)

Meat (pepperoni, ham, hamburger, sausage)

Spinach

Eggplant

Onion

STIR-FRY GARDEN

Stir-fry is a way of cooking foods. It usually refers to a Chinese method of cooking in a wok—a large, shallow, bowl-shaped cooking pan. Lots of different kinds of foods—vegetables and meats—can be heated in a wok. You don't have to use much cooking oil in a wok, and the food is cooked thoroughly and quickly. Stir-fry is limited only by your imagination and taste. Anything that can be boiled or baked can also be stir-fried. And dressed up with a little soy sauce and fresh, grated ginger, almost any combination of vegetables can take on an oriental flair.

Gingerroot is a funny-shaped vegetable found in the produce section of the supermarket. Peel off the glossy sand-colored skin with a paring knife (don't peel the whole root, just the little arm you want to use for the meal), then grate the fresh ginger with a hand-grater, using the smallest holes. This will give your dish a true oriental flavor. A small amount of grated ginger goes a long way in flavoring foods. Two teaspoons of ginger would be plenty for a large wok of vegetables. You can freeze the unused gingerroot in a plastic bag for later use.

You can make your stir-fry more interesting if you use some out-of-the-ordinary vegetables such as snow peas, gingerroot, bean sprouts, yams, mushrooms, and bok choy. Some of these can be difficult to grow because they rely on special conditions—just the right soil, temperature, water, minerals, etc.—so you may have to buy one or two at the store.

But you can grow some stir-fry basics in your garden, and those vegetables can be used in other meals as well.

THE STIR-FRY GARDEN PLAN

If you have a garden space at least as big as a small car, you can plant all the veggies in the boxed list. If your space is smaller than a car, decide which ones are your favorites and just plant those. You can purchase a few other vegetables at a farmer's market to supplement your own garden basics.

THINGS TO GROW
- Green beans
- Carrots
- Sugar pod peas (also called snow peas)
- Zucchini
- Yellow summer squash
- Broccoli
- Onions

If your space is limited, decide whether you want a summer stir-fry or an autumn stir-fry. Plant early-summer crops for a summer stir-fry and late-summer crops for an autumn stir-fry. See the ingredients listed in each recipe below for guidelines, but don't be limited by these. Consult with your adult garden assistant and check the seed packets for the number of days to maturity. This will help you to decide which crops will be ready at about the same time.

RECIPE

UNDERGROUND STIR-FRY

UTENSILS

Large wok or skillet
Long-handled spatula
Lid or splatter guard
Grater
Paring knife
Chef's knife
Cutting board

SUMMER STIR-FRY

Use any or all of these vegetables:

Green onions
Green beans
Sugar pod peas
Zucchini
Yellow summer squash
1/4 cup peanut or canola oil (just enough to keep ingredients from sticking)
Soy sauce
Gingerroot

STEP 1:

COOK THE MEAT

If meat or poultry will be part of your dish, cut it into bite-sized pieces. Pour a little oil in the wok, then add meat and stir-fry on high, turning so each side browns and the meat cooks clear through. Remove meat from pan and set aside while you cook the vegetables.

STEP 2:

PREPARE THE VEGETABLES

Wash and trim the vegetables of your choice. Cut the vegetables into bite-sized pieces and set aside each vegetable in a separate bowl.

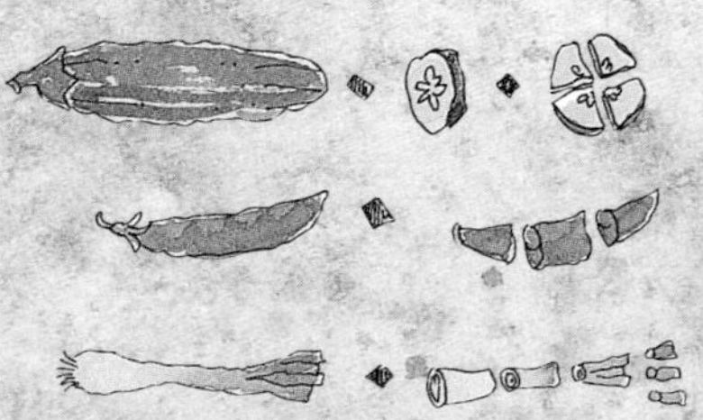

How much of each vegetable? That will depend on how many different kinds you're using and how many servings you want to make. Be sure to estimate how much your wok can hold and still leave enough room for stirring. The more you load into the pan, the longer it will take for the vegetables to cook. Also, it's more difficult to keep a panful of vegetables at an even temperature, so cooking times will vary. Stir-fry tastes best when the vegetables are cooked but not mushy.

STEP 3:

COOK THE VEGETABLES

Add a little oil to the wok, just enough to keep the vegetables from sticking. Place the vegetables in the wok, starting with the longest-cooking

AUTUMN STIR-FRY

Use any or all of these vegetables:

Yellow onions
Carrots
Zucchini
Mushrooms
Yams
Napa cabbage
Broccoli
1/4 cup or less peanut or canola oil
Soy sauce
2 teaspoons sugar
Gingerroot

Add ingredients in this order from the longest-cooking to the shortest-cooking:

Poultry or meat (cook, then set aside)
Onions
Carrots
Yams
Broccoli
Green beans
Sugar pod peas
Zucchini
Summer squash
Napa cabbage
Mushrooms
Bean sprouts

CAUTION: Hot oil splatters, especially when you put the first vegetables in the wok. Use a lid or splatter guard. Work carefully. Use a long-handled spatula for turning the vegetables. Never cook with oil unless an adult helper is present.

vegetables first. With each addition, cook and stir, on high, for 1 to 1-1/2 minutes before adding the next vegetable. (When adding broccoli, it is helpful to add 1/4 cup water and let the broccoli steam a little. This will allow it to cook more evenly, and, with the lid off, the water will evaporate.)

Use the smallest holes.

Before adding the last two vegetables, grate some fresh gingerroot into the wok.

Sprinkle the sugar and some soy sauce (takes the place of salt) over all. Start with a little soy sauce, stir, and let blend for about 1 minute. Then taste a small sample from the wok. If you think it needs more soy sauce, add a little more, but remember: you can always add more soy sauce at the table, but once you've added too much, you can't take it out.

If meat is part of your dish, return it to the wok and stir with the vegetables to reheat before serving.

SPAGHETTI GARDEN

Okay, okay, so you won't be growing the noodles in your windowsill box! But dried spaghetti does come from dirt—it starts out as wheat grown in large fields. So there truly are "spaghetti gardens" being grown all over the countryside right now!

THINGS TO GROW
Roma tomatoes
Zucchini squash
Green peppers
Red peppers
Basil
Oregano
Garlic

You can buy pasta in almost any shape or size. The real fun as a gardener and cook comes in creating the sauce to top your pasta. Spaghetti can be flavored simply by tossing it with olive oil and garlic. It can be smothered with creamy, cheesy concoctions such as an alfredo sauce. Or it can have light, vegetable-based sauces, ranging from a basil-filled pesto sauce to a veggie-filled tomato sauce such as the one in the recipe on page 28.

Almost every Italian cook has his or her own special tomato sauce. The basic

Herbs such as basil and oregano are easy to grow. You can start them as seeds or from plants. When the plants start to flower, that means they are ready to "go to seed," or to quit producing leaves and instead store seeds to start new plants next year. But you can prolong the active life of herb plants by breaking off the flowers. This forces the plant to put its energy into making more leaves, and the plant will actually become bushier. By continuing to snip off new flowers, you can have fresh herbs all summer long.

THE SPAGHETTI GARDEN PLAN

Is the tomato a fruit or vegetable? You might not think that's such an important question. But there was once such a disagreement about it that the United States Supreme Court had to decide! The court ruled in 1893 that the tomato is a vegetable—so don't try to pass any off as an ice-cream sauce!

flavor will depend on the type of tomato used—and there are lots! Because the tomato is so important to the sauce, some cooks will only buy tomatoes at a market the same day they are making their sauce, so that they will have the freshest tomatoes. If yours are a little hard and not a bright red color, you can let them sit on a windowsill in the sun to ripen faster. But many cooks claim that tomatoes ripened on the vine taste best.

RECIPE

SOIL-GROWN SPAGHETTI

UTENSILS

Large skillet (frying pan)

Splatter screen or lid

Long-handled wooden or plastic spatula

Paring knife

Chef's knife

Cutting board

ZIPPY VEGETARIAN SPAGHETTI SAUCE

12 Roma tomatoes

2 small zucchini

1/2 green pepper

1 red pepper

2 cloves garlic

1/3 cup fresh basil leaves (or substitute 1-1/2 teaspoons dry)

1/4 cup fresh oregano leaves (or substitute 1 teaspoon dry)

2 tablespoons olive oil

Salt to taste

FROM THE STORE

1 pound spaghetti or other pasta of your choice

Mushrooms (optional)

Black olives (optional)

Zippy-tasting in your mouth and zippy-cooking on the stove, this is a fast, refreshing alternative to spaghetti sauce in a jar. The sauce takes only 9 or 10 minutes to cook, using just-picked ingredients.

• Prepare the ingredients. Wash all the vegetables in cold water.

• Using a sharp paring knife, cut off and discard the stem ends of the tomatoes, then cube (cut into bite-sized cubes) the tomatoes and set aside.

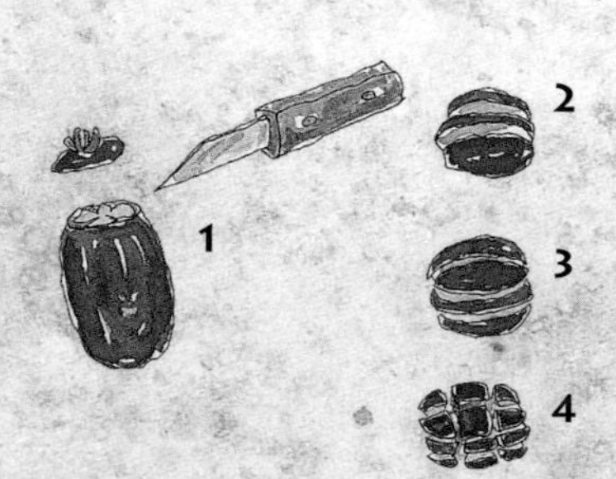

• Cut off both ends of the zucchini, then cut in quarters lengthwise and slice each quarter into small pieces; set aside.

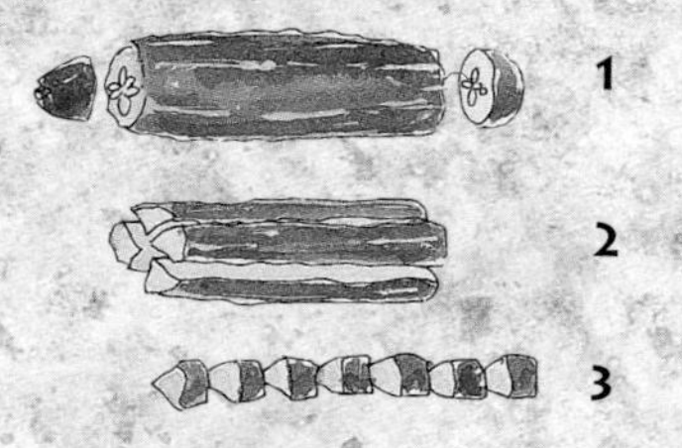

• Clean the peppers, discarding seeds. Cut the peppers into thin strips, then cut the strips in half; set aside.

• Pull the leaves from the basil and oregano stems. Mince (chop into tiny pieces) with a chef's knife (ask an adult to supervise the knife duty) and set aside. Peel the garlic cloves, then mince or crush.

For Italian cooking, *al dente* (all DEN-tay) is an important term to understand. It means "to the tooth," but in cooking means "cooked just enough to retain a firm texture." Italian cooks like their noodles that way—cooked but not mushy. You can feel them when you bite them with your teeth.

This recipe for Zippy Vegetarian Spaghetti Sauce also feels better in your mouth when the vegetables are cooked al dente. The sauce takes only 9 or 10 minutes to cook, so it's a good idea to prepare the vegetables and then stop and cook the spaghetti before starting the sauce. Try turning off the heat under the spaghetti when it's about halfway done. It will finish cooking while it sits in the hot water. This way, you'll be able to get noodles that are cooked *al dente*—just to perfection.

• To cook the sauce, place the garlic in the skillet along with 2 tablespoons olive oil. Turn the heat to medium high and let the oil heat. Be extra careful when cooking with oil. Use a long wooden spatula, and cover the frying pan with a splatter screen to protect yourself from spitting grease. Stir the garlic until it browns just a little. Then add the rest of the ingredients. Cook and stir on medium high for about five minutes, until the peppers and zucchini soften a little. Add salt to taste. Remove from heat and spoon fresh sauce over hot spaghetti noodles. Delicious accompanied by crusty bread and a **Garden Salad** (see page 16).

STUFFED-SPUD GARDEN

THINGS TO GROW
Potatoes
Chives
Broccoli

Had a potato lately? You probably have, since there are so many ways to eat them: baked, with chives and sour cream; boiled, with a little butter; fried, for breakfast; french fried, with ketchup; mashed, with gravy; baked and sliced, with the skins on; and cooked in soups, salads, and even breads.

With so many recipe possibilities, a good gardener will always want to have some potatoes sprouting in the garden. There are lots of varieties of potatoes, too, from your basic brown russet potatoes to new red potatoes to sweet purple potatoes. All of these potatoes can be dressed up in many different ways, so once you get comfortable with the basic potato garden outlined below, you may want to add different ingredients to it, depending on how you like your potatoes.

The good news? Growing potatoes is very little work! Russet is the best variety for baking, but any red or white variety will work fine. Only the texture will vary.

THE STUFFED-SPUD GARDEN PLAN

First, purchase seed potatoes, also called "potato sets." These are potatoes that are cut up so that each piece has an "eye." Using a shovel, dig holes about 6 inches deep, 3 feet apart, and drop one seed into each hole. Pour in about a quart (4 cups) of water, push the dirt back into each hole, and tamp the dirt (to squeeze out the air) by taking one quick, heavy step on top of the dirt. That should do it. Water the potatoes with the rest of your garden. Just wait for the plants to break through the soil, then keep them weeded. The dark green leaves will make lovely green bushes above the ground, but the potatoes are tubers (underground stems), so you won't see them until they are ready to dig.

About 3 to 3-1/2 months from the time you planted them, you will notice the ground around the base of each bush beginning to swell and crack. That's the signal that your potatoes are ready to harvest. At one of the largest cracks, dig away the dirt with your hands and "root" around for a potato. Pull it up. It will be attached to the parent plant by a thin root, or tuber. Just break it off. It will have up to a dozen siblings growing from the same parent plant. So dig a deep, wide circle around the perimeter of each plant, turning the dirt over as you go. Zowie! See how many potatoes you get from one plant? They are all different sizes and shapes. And remember, all you put into the hole was a single "eye."

Store your potatoes in a cool, dry location.

The potato is actually the root part of a plant, growing underground, so when you eat a potato, you really *are* getting your dinner from dirt!

RECIPE

SHOVELED STUFFED SPUDS

UTENSILS
Aluminum foil
Baking sheet
Paring knife
Cutting board
Medium pot with lid

OPTIONAL THINGS TO BUY
Butter
Sour cream
Chili con carne
Bacon bits
Ham
Black olives
Cheese (try different varieties)
Salt and pepper

To prepare potatoes for baking, wash and scrub them with a kitchen brush. Cut away any spoiled parts. Poke a couple of holes through the potato skin with a fork or knife so that air can escape during baking. If you forget to do this, there's a chance your potato might "explode" in the oven.

The surest way to get a happily baked potato is to wrap it in tinfoil. You can bake without foil, too, but the skin will be tougher and drier. Bake potatoes by placing them right on the oven rack for about 1 hour at 350°.

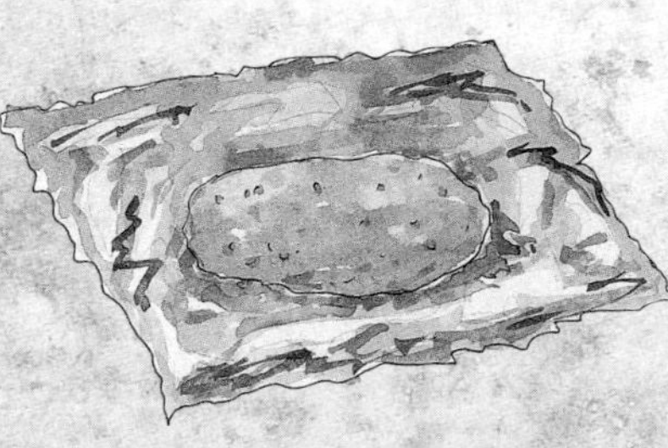

Baking potatoes on the grill is another easy method. Just set the foil-wrapped spuds onto a grill burning at medium-high heat. Check their progress in 30 minutes to estimate how long the cooking will take. Larger potatoes will take longer to cook than smaller ones.

To test for doneness, stick a fork into the potato, right through the foil. If it goes in easily, the spud is ready to eat. If the fork gets stuck partway in, it's a good idea to let your potato cook longer. Test again in 15 minutes.

While the spuds are baking, prepare the broccoli and chives. Cut the desired amounts from plants, then wash in cold water.

Trim the largest leaves from the broccoli stems and cut the broccoli into bite-sized pieces. Place in a pot, add water to a depth of two inches, and turn the stove on high. When the water begins to boil, lower the temperature just enough to keep the water lightly boiling.

Let it boil for five minutes, then turn off the heat and let the broccoli stand in hot water another 5 to 7 minutes. Then drain the water and put the broccoli in a serving bowl.

Cut the chives into pieces about 1/2 inch long. Put in a cup or bowl to serve.

Prepare your other purchased toppers by cutting them into bite-sized pieces, if necessary, and placing them in bowls. When the potatoes are done, you're ready to eat.

Making a stuffed-spud dinner is a lot of fun, especially if you let diners choose their own toppings from the bowls you have set on the table. To make filling the spud easier, give each one a "zigzag cut" before serving. The picture shows how to do this.

Then push both ends toward the center to open a gaping hole in the middle for stuffing in your favorite toppers.

SALSA GARDEN

Think of how many ways you use salsa: for dipping chips, for layering on tacos, and for spreading on hamburgers, just for starters. So a salsa garden is a good basic that will let you use your imagination as a chef. Salsa is generally made up of tomatoes, onions, and peppers, but you can add other ingredients in almost any combination.

THINGS TO GROW

Tomatoes

Cucumbers

Mild yellow chilies

Red onions

Cilantro
(also called coriander)

Garlic

Some store-bought salsa, like some store-bought spaghetti sauce, has a sweet, pasty flavor, not the lighter, more tart flavor that you get when you make your own with garden-fresh tomatoes. Sometimes the stuff in jars has sugars and sauces added to it. The salsa may look thicker and richer, but it may taste pretty flat. If you make your own, you can make it as spicy as you want it.

Fun fact: Salsa is now more popular than ketchup!

THE SALSA GARDEN PLAN

Cilantro may be new to you. It is an herb that gives Mexican dishes a fresh, slightly sweet flavor. Cilantro looks a lot like parsley, but the leaves are bigger. In the garden, it grows like parsley, too—as a bushy green plant. Cilantro grows early in the season, then flowers and goes to seed. (The seeds of the cilantro plant are called coriander and are also used in cooking.) The plant then dries up and dies. You can prolong its season by planting it in partial shade and cutting back (that is, cutting off) the stems about halfway down when you see flower buds start to appear. This forces new leaves to grow on the stems and the plant will bush out again before it goes to seed. (Flowers turn to seeds and drop to the ground, setting the scene for the cilantro plant to grow again next year.)

Cilantro leaves can be used fresh in Mexican dishes. The flavor can be overpowering, so start with a little and add more to suit your taste. Cilantro can also be dried and used in recipes, but the flavor will be much less sweet. Of course, the coriander seeds can be gathered and saved for other recipes not in this book.

RECIPE

SUN-RIPENED SALSA

UTENSILS NEEDED

Vegetable peeler
Chef's knife
Paring knife
Rubber gloves
Cutting board
Medium bowl

Pico de gallo (PEE-koh duh GUY-oh) is a scrumptious summer treat, more fresh-tasting than bottled salsa and especially good with any kind of corn chip—baked or fried, thick or thin, yellow or blue. You'll be surprised at how quickly your friends chow down on this authentic Mexican salsa. The exact balance of tomatoes with other ingredients doesn't matter. Whatever balance tastes right is right for you.

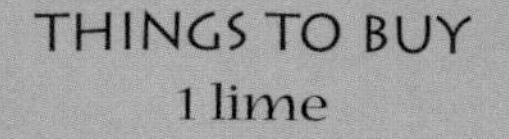

THINGS TO BUY

1 lime

PERKY PICO DE GALLO

5 medium tomatoes, chopped
1/2 cucumber, chopped
1 medium red onion, chopped
2 mild chilies, seeds removed, chopped
1/3 cup cilantro leaves, lightly chopped
1 or 2 garlic cloves, minced
2 tablespoons red wine vinegar
Juice of one lime
1 teaspoon salt, or to taste

Wash all the vegetables and remove the stem ends. Peel the cucumbers before chopping. Working carefully with a chef's knife, cut and chop all the vegetables into pieces no larger in diameter than a dime.

Place the chopped vegetables in a medium bowl as you go. Sprinkle vinegar, lime juice, and salt over all, then toss to mix. Let sit 1 hour in refrigerator, then divide into smaller serving bowls. Scoop up piles of Perky Pico with taco chips, or serve as a topping on hamburgers.

Use extreme caution when working with fresh, uncooked chilies—*this is no joke!* Chilies have an ingredient called capsaicin that burns your skin, eyes, and mouth.

- Never cut a chili unless an adult is supervising.
- Wear kitchen gloves when touching or cutting chilies.
- Don't ever touch a chili and then touch your face or eyes. Even the aroma from a strong chili will burn your eyes and, if inhaled, will make you cough and sputter.

Preparing fresh chilies is a culinary trick but well worth the fuss! The seeds are the hottest part of the chili. With a spoon, scoop out all the seeds and discard before you dice the chilies for the recipe. To prevent accidents, use only mild chilies in this recipe.

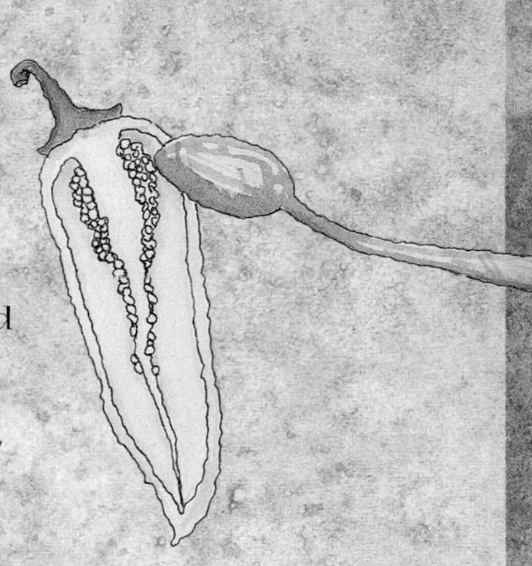

HAMBURGER AND FRIES GARDEN

Your garden won't be sprouting hamburger meat anytime soon, so you'll still have to rely on cattle for that part of the meal (or turkeys, if you like turkey burgers). But what you put on your burger, and what you serve with your burger, can be garden-grown.

You've probably heard people talk about a "balanced" meal. When you're creating a meal, you usually want to serve a good variety of foods—if possible, something from each of the basic food groups (generally, meat and poultry, grains, dairy products, fruits, and vegetables), maybe different colors and textures of foods, maybe foods of different temperatures and tastes. Not only does the variety make the meal more interesting, but your body gets a little bit of all the nutrients it needs to function well. The "balance" comes from not having too much of one thing. The foods you grow in your garden add to that mixture, especially in the vegetable department.

Nothing says "summer" like juicy, red-ripe tomatoes. Homemade burgers are bland without them. Green salads aren't "all they can be" until the tomatoes are added. So what can you do until then? Just practice your summer cuisine. Until you have garden-fresh tomatoes, summer hasn't officially begun.

Tomatoes come in many shapes and even colors. You probably have seen cherry tomatoes, but have you ever seen little pear-shaped tomatoes or tasted a yellow variety? All are delicious. Each variety has its own qualities that make it more suitable for some recipes than others. For burgers, a large tomato that can be sliced thick works best.

THE HAMBURGER-AND-FRIES GARDEN PLAN

THINGS TO GROW

Beefsteak tomatoes (or Big Boy or other large slicing variety)
Leaf lettuce
Cucumbers
Green peppers
Yellow onions

A hamburger-and-fries meal will give you a good balance of foods, from meat to vegetables, hot to cold, crunchy to soft, tart to bland, and bright red to soft brown. And by preparing and growing some foods yourself, you can be sure your hamburger-and-fries meal is a lot more flavorful than one you could buy at a drive-up window!

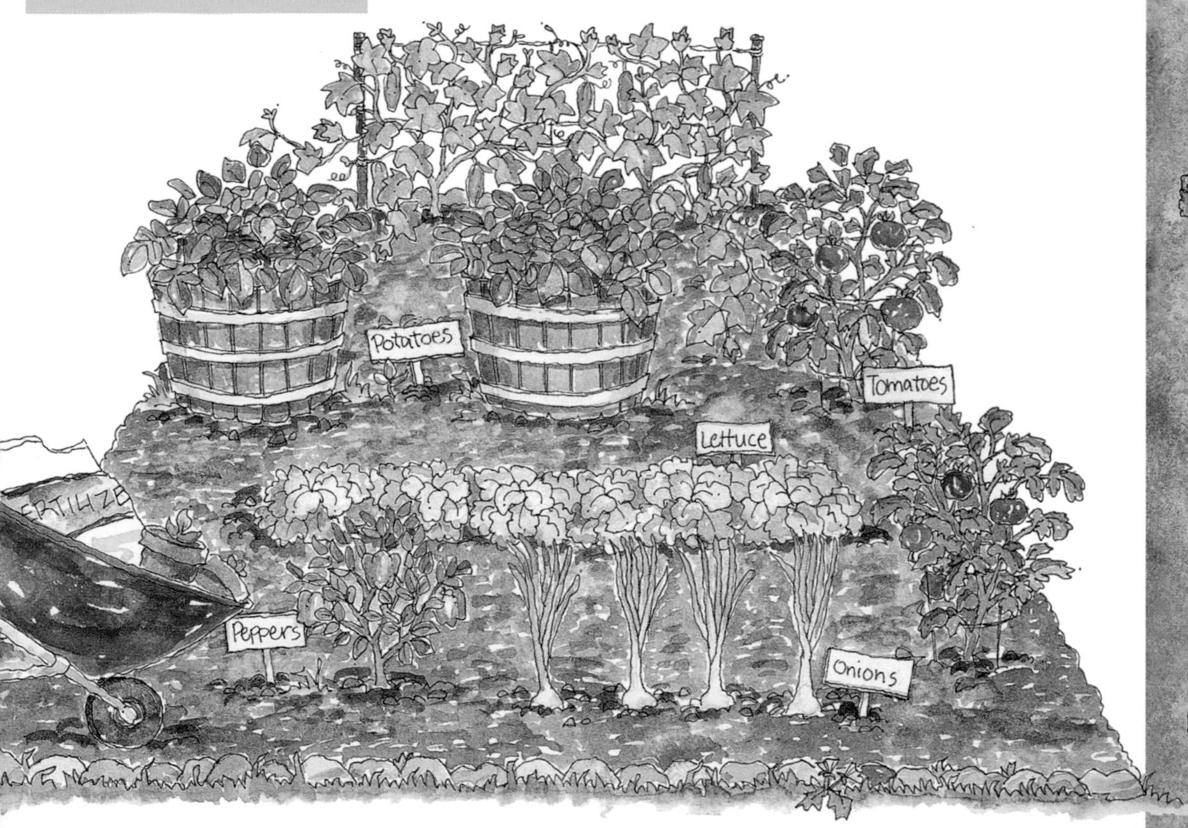

RECIPE

HOE-GROWN HAMBURGER & FRIES

UTENSILS
- Paring knife
- Utility knife
- Medium bowl
- Baking sheet
- Cutting board

THINGS TO BUY
- Meat
- Buns
- Ketchup
- Mustard

Becoming a burger chef at home is as easy as laying things in a stack. First, wash your hands. Then start by forming the ground meat of your choice into round patties, about 1/2-inch thick. Place the burgers in a frying pan on medium-high heat. Cook for about 5 minutes on one side, then carefully flip each patty with a spatula to cook the other side. Make sure the meat is cooked all the way through the middle before removing from heat.

Starting with bread on a plate, layer on any of the following delicious condiments: spreads (such as mustard, ketchup, your favorite dressing), **Perky Pico de Gallo** (see page 36), tomato, green pepper, lettuce, **Dilled Cucumber & Onion Rings**; then meat and bread. Serve with **Country Oven Fries**.

DILLED CUCUMBER AND ONION RINGS

1 cucumber

1/4 yellow onion

2 teaspoons dill weed

1/3 cup vinegar

1/4 cup sugar

Water

Peel a cucumber and slice into rounds about 1/4-inch thick. Cut two or three slices from a yellow onion; separate slices into rings. Place the cucumber and onion slices together in a bowl. Sprinkle with dill weed and sugar, then pour vinegar over all. Add just enough cool water to the bowl to cover the veggies. Cover and let stand in the refrigerator 1–2 hours. Drain the liquid from the bowl, then garnish your hamburger with the "pickled" cucumber and onions. Pass the leftovers as a side dish at the dinner table.

COUNTRY OVEN FRIES

Potato for each diner

Vegetable or canola oil (about 1 tablespoon for each potato)

Salt and pepper to taste

Lightly grease a baking sheet (cookie sheet, pizza pan, or 9 x 13 baking dish). Scrub-a-dub-dub the potatoes (no need to peel), then carefully cut into vertical slices about 1/2-inch thick. Cut each slice into vertical strips about finger width. Place potatoes in a bowl big enough to stir potatoes without spilling. Drizzle oil over fries and toss and turn potatoes to coat with oil. Spread potatoes on a baking sheet. Sprinkle with salt and pepper. Bake at 450° for 15 minutes, then remove baking sheet from oven and turn fries with a spatula. Return to oven and bake 15 minutes more. Remove from the oven and serve hot. Offer ketchup as a condiment.

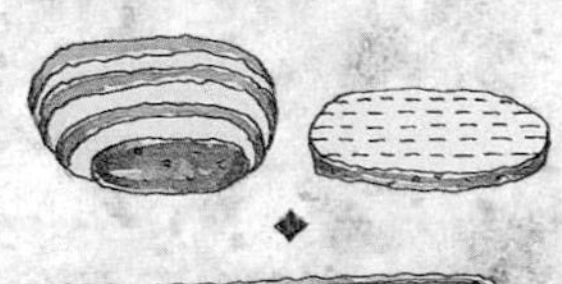

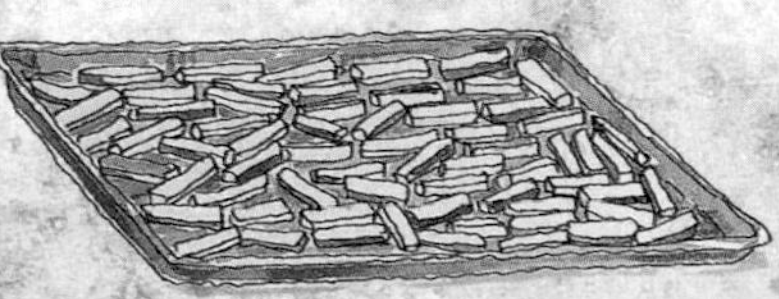

SOUP GARDEN

Soup is a great meal for gardeners *and* cooks (yes, you're both). Many of the ingredients for all kinds of soups can be grown in your garden, and one pot of soup that you leave simmering on the stove for the afternoon makes a meal for your whole family. Soups can be cold summer meals: gazpacho (gauz-PAUCH-oh), for example, is a spicy tomato soup full of vegetables that's refreshing on a warm evening. Soups can be elegant dinner starters; vichyssoise (vi-shee-SWAZ), often served as a cold appetizer, is made with potatoes, cream, and onions or leeks. Some soups make hearty winter meals, such as minestrone, which has vegetables, beans, and pasta in a rich broth. And some people even claim soup can be a cure for the common cold—try good ol' chicken noodle! The basic broth, or stock, you use can be flavored with chicken, beef, vegetables, or fish. The flavor of broth will change the taste of the soup.

THINGS TO GROW

- Tomatoes
- Carrots
- Green beans
- Potatoes
- Chard
- Onions
- Corn
- Zucchini
- Yellow summer squash
- Cabbage

THE SOUP GARDEN PLAN

A soup garden is much more than that. For instance, the tomato plants will produce many tomatoes over the summer, so you can use those for sandwiches, salads, salsa, or other recipes. In the fall, you can use the last of the tomatoes in a hearty Autumn Harvest Soup. Cut the corn off two cobs and save that for soup. Green beans are delicious when steamed, buttered, and sprinkled with dill weed. But save a few for soup also. Carrots can become part of a salad or can be eaten fresh, with a few saved for soup. (Did you know that carrots left in the ground until after the first frost become sweeter than those pulled from the ground before frost?)

Every good chef uses her/his imagination!

Squash
Chard
Beans
Corn

RECIPE

SOUPS FROM SHOOTS

UTENSILS NEEDED

Large covered pot
Long-handled spoon
Cutting board
Paring knife

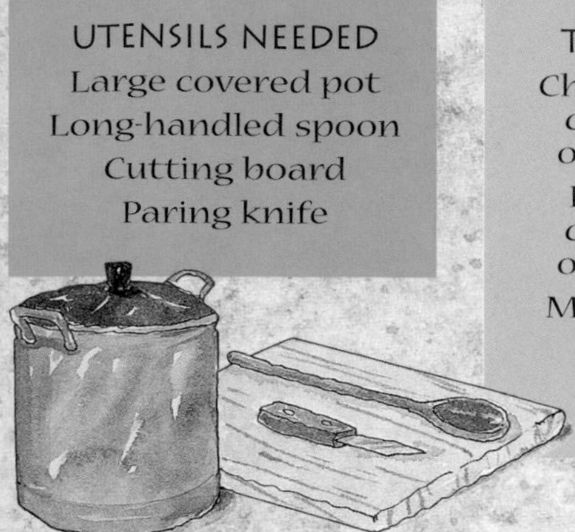

THINGS TO BUY

Chicken boullion—cubes, granules, or canned broth
Beef boullion—cubes, granules, or canned broth
Meat (any variety: leftover roast, stewing beef, or ground beef)

Anything goes in soup. Any vegetables, including bits of leftovers, will only enhance the flavor of a simmered soup supper.

The key to homemade soup is to have a tasty broth base, and that's as easy as opening a jar or box and stirring some instant bouillon into the soup pot. →

LIGHT SUMMER VEGETABLE SOUP

3 carrots, sliced
1 cup green beans, snapped into bite-sized pieces
4 medium potatoes, quartered and sliced
4–6 chard leaves, sliced into thin strips
1 small onion, chopped
1 small zucchini, cut in half and sliced
3/4 cup corn kernels, freshly cut from 2 ears of corn
1 small yellow summer squash, cut in quarters and sliced
6 cups water
3 cubes instant chicken bouillon or 3 teaspoons granules
Salt and pepper to taste

Combine all the ingredients in a medium pot. Cover and bring to a boil. Reduce the heat and simmer for 1 hour, stirring every 10 minutes or so. Taste the broth and adjust the seasonings to suit your taste by adding instant broth or salt and pepper. Be careful not to add too much salt. Serve with French bread for a light and satisfying supper.

Follow the directions on the container for proportions. For instance, if the directions say that 1 boullion cube plus one cup of water makes a cup of broth, then put 1 boullion cube into the soup pot for every cup of water you add. When you taste the soup later, you can always add more boullion if you would like. Or, if the boullion flavor is overpowering, you can add a little water to tone it down.

AUTUMN HARVEST SOUP WITH BEEF

- 2 cups cooked beef, cut into small pieces
- 6 tomatoes, skins removed, chopped, or (1) 16-ounce can tomatoes
- 4 cups water
- 1 medium onion, chopped
- 2 bay leaves
- 1-1/2 cups carrots, diced
- 6 potatoes, diced
- 1 cup cabbage, shredded
- 6 cubes beef bouillon, or 6 teaspoons beef-flavored granules
- Salt and pepper to taste

Combine first five ingredients in a large pot. Cover and bring to a boil. Reduce the heat and simmer for 45 minutes, stirring every 15 minutes. Add the vegetables (carrots, potatoes, cabbage). Bring to a boil, then reduce the heat and let boil lightly for 30 minutes, stirring every 10 minutes.

Taste the broth and adjust the seasonings to suit your taste by adding instant broth or salt and pepper. Remember, the instant broth contains a lot of salt, so add the table salt last and only after tasting. Serve with cornbread or wheat rolls for a hearty autumn main-course supper.

DESSERT GARDEN

What's dinner without dessert? Maybe not worth eating! You probably have a favorite dessert: an ice-cream sundae, maybe, or chocolate cake, or homemade brownies. If you read recipes for different desserts, you might be able to tell which ingredients come from dirt and which don't (chocolate—yes; eggs—no).

THINGS TO GROW
Sugar pumpkins

PUMPKINS
It's hard to imagine that when you drop a pumpkin seed into a hole in the ground, by the end of summer the seed will have grown to a vine that might stretch out to ten feet! Warning: be sure to leave plenty of space between your hills (several seeds planted together in a hole rather than scattered along a row) of pumpkin seeds.

For cooking up delectable pumpkin desserts, the sugar-sweet pumpkin is a tasty variety. It's quite small and easy to handle. But if what you have in mind is a humongous jack-o'-lantern, you can still recycle it right after Halloween for use at the dessert bar.

TO COOK PUMPKIN
Here's how to change a big orange ball into a bowlful of puree (pyur-AY) for use in recipes:

First, scrape out all the seeds. Using a large knife, carefully cut the pumpkin into pieces about the size of a saucer.

Place pieces into a large pot with enough water to almost cover the pumpkin. Cover the pot with a lid and turn on high heat to bring to a boil. Reduce the heat and continue cooking on medium-high until a fork can be easily inserted through the pieces of pumpkin (about 30–40 minutes). Remove the pot from the heat, drain the water, and let cool. When the pumpkin is cool enough to handle, peel the outer skin from the pumpkin with a paring knife. Set the pieces of pumpkin "meat" aside until all are peeled, then puree in a blender.

THE DESSERT GARDEN PLAN

To make puree: Fill a blender half full of pumpkin. Add two tablespoons of water. Blend on medium or high until all the chunks disappear. If the blender binds, turn it off and add more water a tablespoon at a time. Stir the pumpkin with a spatula before turning the blender on again. When pureed, pour the liquid pumpkin into a separate container. Continue processing batches until all the pumpkin is pureed. Any unused pumpkin puree can be frozen.

Be sure to allow plenty of room for your pumpkin plants to grow. They can reach ten feet in length!

RECIPE

DIRTY DESSERTS

UTENSILS NEEDED
Blender
Rubber spatula
Medium bowl
Electric mixer
Wooden spoon
9 x 13 pan

SUGAR 'N' SPICE PUMPKIN BARS

- 1-1/4 cups flour
- 1 cup sugar
- 1/3 cup shortening
- 1 cup pumpkin puree
- 1 teaspoon baking powder
- 2 teaspoons pumpkin-pie spice
- 1/4 cup milk
- 1 teaspoon vanilla
- 1/2 teaspoon baking soda
- 1/2 teaspoon salt
- 2 eggs
- 1/4 cup chopped walnuts
- 1/2 cup powdered sugar

Combine all the ingredients but the powdered sugar in a large bowl. Beat with an electric mixer at medium speed for 2 minutes, or beat for 4 minutes with a wooden spoon. Spread in a 9 x 13 pan that has been oiled and lightly floured. Bake at 375° for 25 to 30 minutes, or until the top springs back when tapped with your fingers. Remove from the oven with hot pads and sprinkle powdered sugar over the top. When cool, cut into squares and serve.

UTENSILS NEEDED
Electric mixer
Large mixing bowl
Measuring spoons
Measuring cups
Tablespoon
Cookie sheet

PUMPKIN CHOCOLATE-CHIP COOKIES

- 1-1/2 cups sugar
- 1/2 cup shortening
- 1 egg
- 1 teaspoon baking powder
- 1 teaspoon baking soda
- 1/2 teaspoon salt
- 1 teaspoon nutmeg
- 1 teaspoon cinnamon
- 1 teaspoon vanilla
- 3 cups flour
- 1-1/2 cups pumpkin puree
- 1 cup raisins
- 1-1/2 cups chocolate chips

Dump all ingredients except the last two into a large bowl. Mix together, then beat for 1-1/2 minutes. Fold in raisins and chocolate chips. Drop by table-spoons onto a greased cookie sheet. Bake at 375° for 10 minutes.